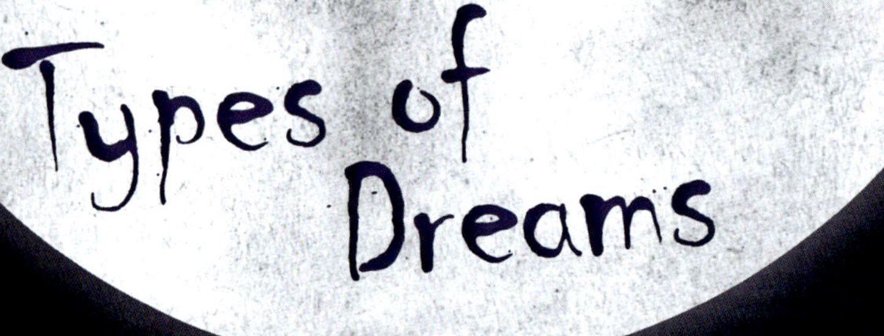

Types of Dreams

There are five main types of dreams:

- normal dreams
- **lucid** dreams – (say: *loo-sid*)
- nightmares
- "waking up" dreams
- daydreams.

In Your Dreams

Dawn McMillan

Contents

While You Are Sleeping

Welcome to the fascinating and strange world of dreams. Dreaming is like thinking when we are asleep. When we dream we think in pictures.

Everybody dreams, but not everybody remembers their dreams. We forget most of our dreams as soon as we wake up.

Another type of dream is a **recurring** dream. This is when we dream the same thing over and over again. Recurring dreams are not as common as other types of dreams.

Normal Dreams

Everybody dreams when they are asleep. We usually dream about things we've been doing or thinking about during the day. Our dreams can also be about things we remember from the past.

We don't know that we are dreaming while we are asleep. Even if the dream is really silly or unbelievable, we think that it's real!

Lucid Dreams

Lucid dreams are when the dreamer knows that they are dreaming. Even though they are asleep, they know what is going on! Lucid dreaming is like being awake in the middle of a dream.

I haven't really finished my homework – I'm just dreaming!

Some people can change or control what is happening in a lucid dream. They can make things disappear and they can change where they are. If they want to start flying, they can do that, too!

Nightmares

Scary dreams are called nightmares. Nightmares are usually about frightening, sad or **unpleasant** things. They often happen when we are frightened, upset or worried about something in real life.

If you have nightmares, talk to someone about them. They may be able to help you understand what is **causing** your nightmares. This should help to solve the problem, and the nightmares should go away.

"Waking Up" Dreams

Sometimes, when you're dreaming you might think you have woken up. You get out of bed and eat your breakfast. You brush your teeth. You even sit down and start to draw.

You haven't woken up though… you're not out of bed and you're not brushing your teeth. You're fast asleep and you're still dreaming! These dreams can be very confusing when you *really* wake up.

Daydreams

Daydreams happen when we are awake. Our minds **wander** and we start to think in pictures. We think of many different things when we daydream – what we want to be when we grow up or what we want for dinner.

Be careful though... daydreaming can get us into trouble if we are supposed to be **concentrating** on something else!

Strangers

Sometimes we might dream about strangers – people we haven't met before. However, these people will not be complete strangers to us. This is because our dreams only show people we have seen before in real life.

Yesterday, we went to the supermarket.

You might not **recognise** your teacher in a dream about school. Instead of the teacher you know, the teacher in your dream could be someone you saw that day, like the lady from the supermarket!

Colours

Do you dream in colour or in black and white? Most people dream in colour or in a mix of colour and black and white.

There are a small number of people who only dream in black and white, even though they see colours when they are awake. Most of these people grew up watching black and white television and movies.

Using Our Senses

We mainly think of dreams as pictures, but all of our senses can play a part. What we hear, smell, taste or touch can also be part of our dreams.

What if you can't see? Do you still dream? People who are blind from birth do dream, but not in pictures. Instead, their dreams are full of sounds, smells, tastes and feelings. For example, a blind person, who is dreaming about the beach, would *hear* the ocean and *feel* the sand between their toes.

Animals

Dogs sleep around 10 to 13 hours a day – that's a lot of dreaming!

Have you ever seen an animal sleeping? It might be twitching or making little sounds. When animals sleep, they dream – just like us! Scientists know that dogs, cats, rats, monkeys, elephants and dolphins all dream.

In fact, scientists know that all **mammals** dream. They also think that birds and **reptiles** dream but that fish and insects don't dream.

What Does It Mean?

Often dreams do not make sense. You might dream about something that is very strange or totally unbelievable. Usually, these types of dreams are about something else – you just have to work out what that is!

Very Strange!

Some artists paint pictures of their dreams.

In your dream, your room might be filled with hundreds of books or a giant pencil! In real life, this might mean that you are worried about finishing your homework!

Write It Down

Most people forget their dreams about 10 minutes after they have woken up. What we remember from our dreams can help us in our everyday lives. This is because our dreams tell us how we are thinking and feeling.

It can be interesting and fun to keep a dream diary. As soon as you wake up, write down what happened in your dreams. This will help you understand what your dreams really mean.

My Dream

Last night, I dreamt I was swimming with dolphins!

Did you know:

- We spend about 1/3 of our lives sleeping.
- We dream for about 1/4 of our sleep time.
- We have about 100 000 dreams in our lives.
- We have 4–7 dreams in one night!

Off you go to sleep…
and dream on!

Glossary

causing	making something happen
concentrating	thinking very hard about something
lucid	clear and easy to understand
mammals	warm-blooded animals
recognise	to know
recurring	happening many times
reptiles	cold-blooded animals
unpleasant	not nice
wander	to roam

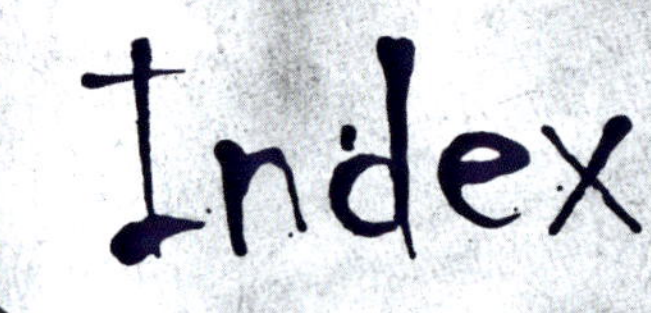

Index